Everybody 's Lonesome

"Both wanted to toast, and they took turns."
(Page 43)

Everybody's Lonesome

A True Fairy Story

By
CLARA E. LAUGHLIN
*Author of "Evolution of a Girl's Ideal,"
"The Lady in Gray," etc.*

Illustrated by
A. I. KELLER

WILDSIDE PRESS

To
Mabel Taliaferro,
The Faery Child

CONTENTS

ILLUSTRATIONS

Everybody 's Lonesome

I

DISAPPOINTED IN LIFE

MARY ALICE came home qui-
etly from the party. Most of
the doors in the house were
closed, because it was cold, and the halls
were hard to heat. Mary Alice knew
exactly what she should see and hear if
she opened that door at her right as she
entered the house, and went into the
sitting-room. There was a soft-coal fire
in the small, old-fashioned grate under
the old, old-fashioned white marble mantel. Dozing—always dozing—on the
hearth-rug, at a comfortable distance

from the fire, was Herod, the big yellow cat. In the centre of the room, under the chandelier, was a table, with a cover of her mother's fancy working, and a droplight with a green shade. By the unbecoming light of this, her mother was sewing. What day was this? Tuesday! She was mending stockings. Mary Alice could see it all. She had been seeing it for twenty years during which nothing— it seemed to her—had changed, except herself. If she went in there now, her mother would ask her the same questions she always asked: "Did you have a nice time?" "Who was there?" "Anybody have on anything new?" "What refreshments did they serve?"

Mary Alice was tired of it all—heartsick with weariness of it—and she stole softly past that closed sitting-room door and up, through the chilly halls where

[10]

she could see her own breath, to her room.

She did not light the gas, but took off in the dark her "good" hat and her "best" gloves and her long black cloth coat of an ugly "store-bought" cut, which was her best and worst. Then, in an abandon of grief which bespoke real desperation in a careful girl like Mary Alice, she threw herself on her bed— without taking off her "good" dress—and buried her head in a pillow, and *hated everything*.

It is hard to be disappointed in love, but after all it is a rather splendid misery in which one may have a sense of kinship with earth's greatest and best; and it has its hopes, its consolations. There is often the hope that this love may return; and, though we never admit it, there is always—deep down—the consolation of believing that another and a better may come.

But to be disappointed in the love of life is not a splendid misery. And Mary Alice was disappointed in her love of life. To be twenty, and not to believe in the fairies of Romance ; to be twenty and, instead of the rosy dreams you've had, to see life stretching on and on before you, an endless, uninspired humdrum like mother's, darning stockings by the sitting-room fire—that is bitterness indeed.

Hardship isn't anything—while you believe in life. Stiff toil and scant fare are nothing—while you expect to meet at any turning the Enchanter with your fortune in his hands. But to be twenty and not to believe —— !

Mary Alice had never had much, except the wonderful heart of youth, to feed her faith with. She wasn't pretty and she wasn't clever and she had no accomplishments. Her people were "plain" and perpetually "pinched" in circumstance. And her life, in this small town where she lived, was very narrow.

In the mornings, Mary Alice helped her mother with the housework. In the afternoons, after the midday dinner was cleared away, Mary Alice had a good deal of time on her hands. Sometimes she sewed—made new clothes or remade old ones ; sometimes she read. Once in a while she took some fancy work and went to see a girl friend, or a girl friend brought some fancy work and came to see her. Occasionally she and another girl went for a walk. Semi-occasionally there was a church social or a sewing circle luncheon, or somebody gave a party.

Somebody had given a party to-day,

and Mary Alice had gone to it with high hope of finding it "interesting" and had come away from it with a deep despair of ever finding in life that which would make the monotony of it worth while.

Many another girl, feeling as Mary Alice did, would have gone away from home seeking "life" in a big city. But Mary Alice, besides having no qualifications for earning her way in a big city, had a most unhappy shyness. She was literally afraid of strangers, and never got very well acquainted even with persons she had associated with for a long time.

At the party to-day—it was an afternoon tea—Mary Alice had been more bitterly conscious than ever before of her lack of charms and the bleak prospect that lack entailed upon her. For the tea was given for a girl who was visiting in town, a girl of a sort Mary Alice had never seen before. She was pretty, that visiting girl, and she was sweet; she had a charm that was irresistible; she seemed to like everybody, and there was no mistake about everybody liking her. Even the town girls liked her and were not jealous. Even Mary Alice liked her, and was not afraid of her. But there she was —that girl!—vital, radiant, an example of what life might be, at twenty. And Mary Alice came away hating as she had never done before, life as it was for her and as it promised to continue.

Presently she withdrew her head from the pillow and lay looking into the dark where, as we all know, the things that might be, that should have been, shape themselves so much more readily than in any light. And, lying there, Mary Alice wondered if there were any fairy power on earth that could make of her a being half so sweet as that girl she had seen this afternoon.

Then she heard her mother open the sitting-room door and call her. It was time to get their simple supper ready.

"In a minute!" she called back. "I'm changing my dress." And she jerked at the hooks of her blue taffeta "jumper dress" with uncareful haste; bathed her face in cold water; put on her dark red serge which had been "good" last year; and went down-stairs to help her mother.

She could see it all as she went—all she was to do. There was the threadbare blanket they used for a silence cloth, and the table-cloth with the red stain by Johnny's place where he had spilled cranberry jelly the night before last, when the cloth was "span clean." There were the places to set, as always, with the same old dishes and the same old knives and forks ; and with the mechanical precision born of long practice she would rightly place, without half looking at them, the various napkins each in its slightly different wooden ring. The utmost variety that she could hope for would be hot gingerbread instead of the last of Sunday's layer-cake, and maybe frizzled beef, since they had finished Sunday's roast in a meat pie this noon.

"I didn't hear you come in," said her mother as Mary Alice opened the sitting-room door, "and I was listening for you."

"I went right up-stairs to change my things," said Mary Alice, hoping that would end the matter.

"That's what I knew you must have done when it got to be six o'clock and I didn't hear you. I could hardly wait for you to come. I've such a surprise for you."

Mary Alice could hardly believe her ears. "A surprise?" she echoed, incredulously.

"Yes. I got a letter this afternoon from your dear godmother."

"Oh!" Mary Alice's tone said plainly: Is that all? She had her own opinion of her godmother, whom she had not seen since she was a small child, and it was not an enthusiastic one. Her name— which she hated—was her godmother's name. And aside from that, all she had ever got from her godmother was an occasional letter and, on Christmas and birthdays, a handkerchief or turnover collar or some other such trifle as could come in an envelope from Europe where her godmother lived.

Even in the matter of a godmother, it seemed, it was Mary Alice's luck to have one without any of the fairy powers.

Disappointed in Life

For although Mary Alice's mother had dearly loved, in her girlhood, that friend for whom she had called her first baby, she had always to admit, to Mary Alice's eager questioning, that the friend was neither beautiful nor rich nor gifted. She was a "spinster person" and years ago some well-to-do friend had taken her abroad for company. And there she had stayed; while the friend of her girlhood, whose baby was called for her, heard from her but desultorily.

"Your godmother has come back," said Mary Alice's mother, her voice trembling with excitement; "she's in New York. And she wants you to come and see her."

For a moment, visions swam before Mary Alice's eyes. Then, "How kind of her!" she said, bitterly; and turned away.

Her mother understood. "She's sent a check!" she cried, waving it.

After that, until Mary Alice went, it was nothing but talk of clothes and other ways and means. Just what the present circumstances of Godmother were, they could not even conjecture; but they were probably not very different than before, or she would have said something about them. And the check she sent covered travelling expenses only. Nor did she write: Never mind about clothes; we will take care of those when she gets here.

"I haven't the least idea what kind of a time you'll have," Mary Alice's mother said, "but you mustn't expect many parties or much young society. Your godmother has been abroad so long, she can't have many acquaintances in this

country now. But you'll see New York
—the crowds and the shops and the
great hotels and the places of historic
interest. And even if you don't meet
many people, you'll probably have a
very interesting time."

"I don't care about people, anyway,"
returned Mary Alice.

Her mother looked distressed. "I
wouldn't say that, if I were you," she
advised. "Because you *want* to care
about people—you *must!* Sights are
beguiling, but they're never satisfying.
We all have to depend on people for our
happiness—for love."

"Then I'll never be happy, I guess,"
said Mary Alice.

"I'm afraid, sometimes, that you've
started out not to be," her mother answered, gravely, "but we'll hope for the
best."

II

YOUR OWN IS WAITING

MARY ALICE dreaded to meet her godmother. The excitement of getting away
was all very well. But once she was
alone in the Pullman, and the friendly
faces on the station platform were left
behind, she began to think apprehen-
sively of what she was going to. She
was sure to feel "strange" with her godmother, and there was at least a pretty
good chance that she might actually dis-
like her. Also, there was every reason
to doubt if her godmother would like
Mary Alice. Mary Alice had several
times met persons who had "been to
Europe," and she had never liked them;
their conversation was all about things

[22]

she did not know, and larded with phrases she could not understand. Those years in Europe made her doubly dread her godmother.

But the minute she saw her godmother at the Grand Central Station, she liked her; and before they had got home, in the Fourth Avenue car, she liked her very much; and when she lay dozing off to sleep, that first night in New York, she was blissfully conscious that she loved her godmother.

Godmother lived in an apartment in Gramercy Park. It was an old-fashioned apartment, occupying one floor of what had once been a handsome dwelling of the tall "chimney" type common in New York. All around the Square were the homes of notable persons, and clubs frequented by famous men. Godmother was to point these out in the morning;

[23]

but this evening, before dinner was served, while she and Mary Alice were standing in the window of her charming drawing-room, she showed which was The Players, and indicated the windows of the room where Edwin Booth died. It seemed that she had known Edwin Booth quite well when she was a girl, and had some beautiful stories of his kindness and his shyness to tell.

Mary Alice was surprised and delighted, and she looked over at the windows with eager, shining eyes. "He must have been wonderful to know," she said. "Do you suppose there are many other great people like that?"

"A good many, I should say," her godmother replied. And as they sat at dinner, served by Godmother's neat maid-of-all-work, it "kind o' came out," as Mary Alice would have said, how many delightful people Godmother had counted among her friends.

"You've had a beautiful time, all your life, haven't you?" Mary Alice commented admiringly, when they were back in the cozy drawing-room and Godmother was serving coffee from the copper percolator.

"Not all my life, but most of it—yes," said Godmother. "It took me some time to find the talisman, the charm, the secret —or whatever you want to call it—of having a happy time."

"But you found it?"

Godmother flushed as if she were a little bit embarrassed. "Well," she said, "I found one—at last—that worked, for me."

"I wish I could find one," sighed Mary Alice, wistfully.

"I'm going to try to give you mine,"

said Godmother, "or at least to share it with you. And all I ask of you is, that if it 'works' for you, you'll pass it on to some one else."

"Oh, I will!" cried Mary Alice. "What is it?"

"Wait a minute! I have to tell you about me, first—so you'll understand."

"Please do!" urged Mary Alice. "I'd love to hear."

"Well, you see, when the invitations to my christening were sent out, my folks forgot the fairies, I guess. And as I grew up, I found that I hadn't been gifted with wealth or beauty or talents or charm——"

"I know," Mary Alice broke in.

Godmother looked surprised.

"I mean, I know how that feels," Mary Alice explained.

"Then you know I was pretty unhappy until—something happened. I met a charming woman, once, who was so sweet and sympathetic that my heart just opened to her as flowers to sunshine; and I told her how I felt. 'Well, that *was* an oversight!' she said, 'but you know what to do about it, don't you?' I said I didn't. 'Why!' she said, 'the fairies had their gifts all ready to bring, and when they were not invited to the party, what would they naturally do?' 'Give them to some one else!' I cried. I shall never forget how reproachfully she looked at me. 'That is a purely human trick!' she said; 'fairies are never guilty of it. When they have something for you, they keep it for you till you get it. If they were not asked to your party, it's your business to hunt them out and get your gifts. Somewhere in the world your own is waiting for you.' That was a magic thought: Somewhere in the world your own is waiting for you. I couldn't get away from it; it filled my mind, waking and asleep. And I set out to find if it was true."

" And *was* it?"

" Well, it must have been. For I've found some of my own, surely, and I believe I shall find more. And oh! the joy it is to look and look, believing that you will surely find. I haven't found wealth, nor beauty, nor accomplishments —perhaps I didn't look in the right places for any of those—but I've found something I wouldn't trade for all the others. It is all I have to bequeath you, dear. But the beautiful part of this bequest is, I don't have to die to enrich you with it, nor do I have to impoverish myself to give it away. I just whisper something in your ear—and then you go and see if it isn't so."

[28]

"Whisper it now, please," begged Mary Alice, going over to her god-mother and putting her ear close.

"Oh, no," said Godmother, kissing Mary Alice's ear, "this isn't the time at all. And it's *fatal* to tell till the right time comes."

And no teasing would avail to make her change her mind.

III

FINDING THE FIRST FAIRY

THE next few days were spent in sightseeing; and Mary Alice would never
have believed there could be any one so
enchanting to see sights with as Godmother. They looked in all the wonderful shop-windows and "chose" what
they would take from each if a fairy suddenly invited them to take their choice.
No fairy did; but they hardly noticed that.

Then they'd go and "poke" in rem-
nant boxes on the ends of counters in the
big department stores, and unearth bits
of trimming and of lace with which
Godmother, who was clever with her
needle and "full of ideas," showed Mary
Alice how to put quite transforming
touches on her clothes.

They visited art galleries, and Godmother knew things about the pictures
that made them all fascinating. Instead
of saying, " Interesting composition,
that ! " or " This man was celebrated for
his chiaroscuro," Godmother was full of
human stories of the struggles of the
painters and their faithfulness to ideals ;
and she could stand in front of a canvas
by almost any master, and talk to Mary
Alice about the painter and the condi-
tions of his life and love and longing
when he painted this picture, in a way
that made Mary Alice feel as if she'd
like to *shake* the people who walked by
with only an uninterested glance ; as if
she'd like to bring them back and prod
them into life, and cry, " Don't you see ?
How *can* you pass so carelessly what
cost so much in toil and tears ? "

Godmother had that kind of a view-

point about everything, it seemed.
When they went to the theatre, she
could tell Mary Alice—before the curtain
went up, and between the acts—such
things about the actors and the play-
wright and the manager, as made the
play trebly interesting.

On the East Side they visited some of
the Settlements and " prowled " (as Godmother loved to call it) around the teem-
ing slums ; and Godmother knew such
touching stories of the Old World condi-
tions from which these myriads of foreign folk had escaped, and of the pathos
of their trust in the New World, as kept
Mary Alice's eyes bright and wet almost
every minute.

One beautiful sunny afternoon they
rode up on top of a Fifth Avenue motor
'bus to 90th Street, and Godmother
pointed out the houses of many multi-

millionaires. She knew things about many of them, too—sweet, human, heart-touching things about their disappointments and unsatisfied yearnings— which made one feel rather sorry for them than envious of their splendours.

Thus the days passed, and Mary Alice was so happy that—learning from Godmother some of her pretty ways—she would go closer to that dear lady, every once in a while, and say: "Pinch me, please—and see if I'm awake; if it's really true." And Godmother always pinched her, gravely, and appeared to be much relieved when Mary Alice cried "Ouch! I *am!*"

They didn't see anybody, except "from a distance" as they said, for fully a week; they were so busy seeing sights and getting acquainted. Every night when Godmother came to tuck Mary Alice in,

they had the dearest talks of all. And
every night Mary Alice begged to be
told the Secret. But, "Oh, dear no! not
yet!" Godmother would always say.

One night, however, she said: "Well,
if I'm not almost forgetting to tell you!"

Mary Alice jumped; that sounded like
the Secret. But it wasn't—although it
was "leading up to it."

"Tell me what?" she cried, excitedly.

"Why, to-day I saw one of your
fairies."

"My what?"

"Your fairies that you said were left
out of your christening party."

"You did! Where?"

"I'll tell you that presently. But it
seems, from what this fairy said, that
there are a great number of your fairies
with gifts for you, all waiting quite im-
patiently to be found. She says that it

is considered quite 'ordinary' now, to send all of a great gift by one fairy—yes, and not at all safe. For if that one fairy should miss you and you should not find her, you'd be left terribly unprovided for, you see. So the gift is usually divided into many parts, and a different fairy has each part. Now, the gift of beauty, for instance; she is one of the fairies who has that gift for you."

Mary Alice's eyes opened wide. Her belief in this wonderful Godmother was such that she was almost prepared to see Godmother wave a wand and command her to become beautiful—and then, on looking into a mirror, to find that she was so. "What did she say?" she managed at last to gasp.

"She said: 'Has she pretty hair?' And I answered, 'Yes.' 'Then,' the fairy went on, 'the one who had that gift must

[35]

have got to the christening, somehow. Maybe the mother wished for her—and that is as good as an invitation.'"

"She did!" cried Mary Alice. "She's always said she watched me so anxiously when I was a wee baby, hoping I'd have pretty hair."

"Well, that's evidently how that fairy got to you. But it seems there were two. This one I saw to-day says there are two beauties in 'most everything—but especially in hair—one is in the thing itself and the other is in knowing what to do with it. It seems she is the 'what to do' fairy."

And so she proved to be. For, when she came to luncheon next day, she told Mary Alice how she had always been "a bit daft about hair." "When I played with my dolls," she said, "I always cared much more for combing their hair and

doing it up with mother's 'invisible' pins,
than for dressing them. And it used to
be the supreme reward for goodness when
I could take down my mother's beautiful
hair and play with it for half an hour.
I'm always wanting to play with lovely
hair. And when I saw yours at the
theatre the other evening, I couldn't rest
until I'd asked your godmother if she
thought you'd let me play with it."

So after luncheon they went into Mary
Alice's room and wouldn't let Godmother
go with them. "Not at all!" said the
"what to do fairy," "you are the select
audience. You go into the drawing-
room and 'compose yourself.' When
we're ready for you, we'll come out."

Then, behind locked doors, with much
delightful nonsense and excitement, she
divested Mary Alice's head of sundry aw-
ful rats and puffs, combed out the bunches

which Mary Alice wore in her really lovely hair, brushed smooth the traces of the curling iron, and then made Mary Alice shut her eyes and "hope to die" if she "peeked once."

When permission to "peek" was given, Mary Alice didn't know herself.

"There!" said the fairy, when the excitement of Godmother's delight had subsided, "I've always said that the three most important beauty fairies for a girl to find are the how-to-stand fairy, the how-to-dress fairy, and the what-to-do-with-your-hair fairy. Anybody can find them all; and nobody who has found them all needs to feel very bad if she can't find some of the others who have her christening gifts."

Mary Alice began looking for the others, right away. But even one fairy had transformed her, outside, from an ordi-

nary-looking girl into a young woman
with a look of remarkable distinction;
just as Godmother had transformed her,
within, from a girl with a dreary outlook
on life, to one who found that

" The world is so full of a number of things,
I'm sure we should all be as happy as kings."

"Is this the Secret?" she asked Godmother, that night.

"Oh, dear, no!" laughed Godmother,
"only the first little step towards realiz-
ing it."

IV

BEING KIND TO A TIRED MAN

ONE day when Mary Alice had been in New York nearly two weeks—and had found several fairies—Godmother was obliged to go out, in the afternoon, to some sort of a committee meeting which would have been quite uninteresting to an outsider. But Mary Alice had some sewing to do—something like taking the ugly, ruffly sleeves of cheap white lace out of her blue taffeta dress and substituting plain dark ones of net dyed to match the silk ; and she was glad to stay at home.

"If an elderly gentleman comes in to call on me, late in the afternoon but before I get back home," said Godmother,

in departing, "ask him in and be nice
to him. He's a lonely body, and he'll
probably be tired. He works very
hard."

Mary Alice promised, and went happily
to work on the new sleeves which were
to give her arms and shoulders something
of an exquisite outline, in keeping with
the fairy way of doing her hair, which
Godmother had taught her to admire in
a beautiful marble in the Metropolitan
Museum.

About five o'clock, when Godmother's
neat little maid had just lighted the lamps
in the pretty drawing-room and replen-
ished the open fire which was one of the
great compensations for the many draw-
backs of living in an old-fashioned house,
the gentleman Godmother had expected
called.

Mary Alice went in to see him, and ex-

plained who she was. He said he had
heard about her and was glad to make
her acquaintance.

He seemed quite tired, and Mary Alice
asked him if he had been working hard
that day.

"Yes," he said, "very hard."

"Wouldn't you like a cup of tea?" she
asked. And he said he would.

When the tea came, he seemed to enjoy it so much that Mary Alice really
believed he was hungry. Indeed, he
admitted that he was. "I haven't had
any luncheon," he said.

Mary Alice's heart was touched; she
forgot that the man was strange, and
remembered only that he was tired and
hungry.

The little maid brought thin slices of
bread and butter with the tea. Mary
Alice felt they must seem absurd to a

hungry man. "I know what's lots nicer with tea," she said.

"What?" he asked, interestedly

"Toast and marmalade," she answered. "I'm going to get some." And she went to the kitchen, cut a plateful of toasting slices and brought them back with a long toasting fork and a jar of orange marmalade.

"At home," she said, "we often make the toast for supper at the sitting-room fire, and it's *much* nicer than 'gas range toast.'"

"I know it is," he said; "let's do it."

So they squatted on the rug in front of the open fire. Both wanted to toast, and they took turns.

"I don't get to do anything like this very often—only when I come here," he said, apologizing for accepting his turn when it came.

"Don't you live at home?" asked Mary Alice.

"Well, no," he answered, "I'd hardly call what I do 'living at home.'"

There was something about the way he said it that made Mary Alice feel sorry for him; but she didn't like to ask any more questions.

They had a delightful time. Mary Alice had never met a man she enjoyed so much. He liked to "play" as much as Godmother did, and they talked most confidentially about their likes and dislikes, many of which seemed to be mutual. Mary Alice admitted to him how she disliked to meet strangers, and he admitted to her that he felt the very same way.

Godmother tarried and tarried, and at six o'clock the gentleman said he must go.

Being Kind to a Tired Man

"Oh, dear!" sighed Mary Alice. "I'm sorry! I'm having *such* a nice time."

"So am I," he echoed gallantly, "but I'm hoping you will ask me again."

"Indeed I will!" she cried. "We seem to—to get on together beautifully."

"We do," he agreed, "and if it's a rare experience for you, I don't mind telling you it is for me too."

He couldn't have been gone more than ten minutes when Godmother came in.

"That gentleman called," Mary Alice told her. "He's just gone. We had a lovely time."

"I know," said Godmother, "I met him down-stairs and we've been chatting. He says he doesn't know when he's spent a pleasanter hour."

"Poor man!" murmured Mary Alice, "he seems to be a lonely body."

"He is," said Godmother. "He likes to come in here, once in a while, for a cup of tea and an hour's chat. And I'm always glad to have him."

"I should think so!" agreed Mary Alice. "He ate nearly a whole plate of toast."

Godmother laughed so heartily that Mary Alice was a little mystified. She didn't see the joke in being hungry. She didn't even see it when Godmother told her who the man was.

"Not really?" gasped Mary Alice. Godmother nodded. "Why, he told me him*self*——!" Mary Alice began; and then stopped to put two and two together. It was all very astounding, but there was no reason why what he had told her and what Godmother said might not both be true.

"If I had *known!*" she said, sinking

[46]

down, weak in the knees, into the nearest chair.

"That was what gave him his happy hour," said Godmother. "You didn't know! It is so hard for him to get away from people who know—to find people who are able to forget. That's why he likes to come here; I try to help him forget, for an hour, once in a while, at 'candle-lightin' time.'"

"I see," murmured Mary Alice.

The man was one of those great world-powers of finance whose transactions filled columns of the newspapers and were familiar to almost every school child.

That night when Godmother was tucking Mary Alice in, they had a long, long talk about the caller of the afternoon and about some other people Godmother knew, and about how sad a thing it is to take for granted about any person certain qualities we think must go with his estate.

"And now," said Godmother, "I'm going to tell you the Secret."

And she did. Then turned out the light, kissed Mary Alice one more time, and left her to think about it.

V

GOING TO THE PARTY

"Now," said Godmother, the very next morning after she had told Mary Alice the Secret, "to see how it *works!* This evening I am going to take you to a most delightful place."

"What kind of a place?" Mary Alice begged to know. Already, despite the Secret, she was feeling fearful.

Godmother squeezed Mary Alice's hand sympathetically; and then, because that was not enough, she dropped a brief kiss on Mary Alice's anxious young forehead. "I know how you feel, dear," she whispered. "All of us, I guess, have fairy charms that we're afraid to use. Others have used them, we know, and found them miraculous. But somehow, we're afraid. I'm all undecided in my mind whether to tell you about this place we're going to, or not to tell you about it. I want to do what is easiest for you. Now, you think! It probably won't be a very large assembly. These dear people, who have many friends, are at home on Friday evenings. Sometimes a large number call, sometimes only a few. And in New York, you know, people are not 'introduced round'; you just meet such of your fellow guests as happen to 'come your way,' so to speak. That is, if there are many. We'll go down and call this evening—take our chance of few or many, and try out our Secret. And I'll do just as you think you'd like best; I'll tell you about the people we're going to see and try to guess as well as I can who else may be there. Or I won't tell you

anything at all—just leave you to remember that 'folks is folks,' and to find
out the rest for yourself. You needn't
decide now. Take all day to think
about it, if you like."

"Oh, dear!" cried Mary Alice, "I'm
all in a flutter. I don't believe I'll ever
be able to decide, but I'll think hard all
day. And now tell me what I am to
wear."

She went to her room and got her
dark blue taffeta and showed the prog-
ress of yesterday with the new dark net
sleeves to replace the ugly ruffly white
lace ones.

"That's going to be fine!" approved
Godmother. "Now, this morning I am
going to help you make the new yoke
and collar; and then"—she squinted up
her eyes and began looking as if she
were studying a picture the way so many

[51]

picture-lovers like to do, through only a narrow slit of vision which sharpens perspective and intensifies detail—"I think we'll go shopping. Yesterday, when I was hurrying past and hadn't time to stop for longer than a peek, I saw in a Broadway shop-window some short strings of pink imitation coral of the most adorable colour, for—what do you think? Twenty-five cents a string! I've a picture of you in my mind, with your dark blue dress and one of those coral strings about your throat."

Godmother's picture looked very sweet indeed when she came out to dinner that evening. It was astonishing how many of her fairies Mary Alice had found in two short weeks! The lovely lines of her shoulders, which she had never known were the chief of all the "lines of beauty," were no longer disfigured by stiff, out-

standing bretelles and ruffled-lace sleeves,
but revealed in all their delicate charm
by the close-fitting plain dark net. And
above them rose the head of such unsus-
pected loveliness of contour, which rats
and puffs and pompadour had once de-
formed grotesquely, but which the wonderful new hair-dressing accentuated in a
transfiguring degree. The poise of Mary
Alice's head, the carriage of her shoulders, were fine. But she had never known,
before, that those were big points of
beauty. So she *did* look lovely, with the
tiny touch of coral at her throat, the pink
flush in her cheeks, and the sparkle of
excitement in her eyes. It was her first
" party " in New York, and she and Godmother had had the most delicious day
getting ready for it. Mary Alice couldn't
really believe that all they did was to fix
over her blue " jumper dress " and invest

twenty-five cents in pink beads. But it seemed that when you were with a person like Godmother, what you actually did was magnified a thousandfold by the enchanting way you did it. Mary Alice was beginning to see that a fairy wand which can turn a pumpkin into a gold coach is not exceeded in possibilities by a fairy mind which can turn any ordinary, commonplace, matter-of-fact thing into a delightful "experience."

But something had happened during the afternoon which decided what to do about the party. They were walking west in Thirty-Third Street, past the Waldorf, when a lady came out to get into her auto. Godmother greeted her delightedly and introduced Mary Alice. But the lady's name overpowered Mary Alice and completely tied her tongue during the moment's chat.

Going to the Party

"I used to see her a great deal, in Dresden," said Godmother when they had gone on their way, "and she's a dear. We must go and see her as she asked us to, and have her down to see us." Godmother spoke as if a very celebrated prima donna at the Metropolitan Opera were no different from any one else one might happen to know. Mary Alice couldn't get used to it.

"I—I guess I manage better when I don't know so much," she said, smiling rather wofully and remembering the man of many millions to whom she had been "nice" because she thought he was homeless and hungry.

So to the "party" they went and never an inkling had Mary Alice where it was to be or whether she was to see more captains of finance or more nightingales of song, "or what."

VI

THE "LION" OF THE EVENING

THE house they entered was not at all pretentious. It was an old-fashioned house in that older part of New York in which Godmother herself lived—only further south. But it was a remodelled house; the old, high "stoop" had been taken away, and one entered, from the street level, what had once been a basement dining-room but was now a kind of reception hall. Here they left their wraps in charge of a well-bred maid whom Godmother called by name and seemed to know. And then they went up-stairs. Mary Alice was "all panicky inside," but she kept trying to remember the Secret.

Their hostess was a middle-aged lady,

very plain but motherly-looking. She wore her hair combed in a way that would have been considered "terribly old-fashioned" in Mary Alice's home town, and she had on several large cameos very like some Mary Alice's mother had and scorned to wear.

Mary Alice was reasonably sure this lady was not "a millionairess or anything like that," and she didn't think she was another prima donna. The lady's name meant nothing to her.

"Well," their hostess said as Godmother greeted her, "now the party *can* begin—here's Mary Alice! *Two* Mary Alices!" she added as she caught sight of the second one. "Who says this isn't going to be a real party?"

Evidently they liked Godmother in this house; and evidently they were prepared to like Mary Alice. Then, before she had

[57]

time to think any more about it, three or
four persons came up to greet Godmother,
who didn't try to introduce Mary Alice at
all—just let her "tag along" without any
responsibility.

Mary Alice found that she liked to hear
these people talk. They had a kind of
eagerness about many things that made
them all seem to have much more to say
than could possibly be said then and
there. Mary Alice felt just as she thought
the lady must have felt who, after the
man standing beside Mary Alice had made
one or two remarks, in a brief turn the
conversation took towards the Children's
Theatre, cried : "Oh ! I want to talk to
you about that." And they moved away
somewhere and sat down together. Then,
somehow, from that the general talk
glanced off on to some actors and ac-
tresses who had come out of the foreign

quarter where the Children's Theatre was, and were astonishing up-town folk with the fire and fervour of their art. Some one who seemed to know a good deal about the speaking voice, commented on the curious change of tone, from resonant throat sounds to nasal head sounds, which generally marked the Slav's transition from his native tongue to English; and gave several examples in such excellent imitation that every one was amused, even Mary Alice, who knew nothing about the persons imitated.

Then, some one who had been recently to California and seen Madame Modjeska and been privileged to hear some chapters of the memoirs she was writing, told an incident or two from them about the experiences of that great Polish artiste in learning English. A man asked this lady if she knew what Modjeska was

going to do with her Memoirs when they
were ready for publication; and they
two moved away to talk more about
that. And so it went. Mary Alice
didn't often know what the talk was
about; but she was so interested in it
that she found herself wishing they would
talk more about each thing and wouldn't
break up and drift off the way they did.
They had such a wide, wide world—these
people—and they seemed to see everything that went on around them, to feel
everything that can go on within. And
they made no effort about anything.
They talked about the Red Cross cam-
paign against tuberculosis, or big game
hunting in Africa, or the unerring accu-
racy of steel-workers on the skeletons of
skyscrapers, throwing red-hot rivets
across yawning spaces and striking the
bucket, held to receive them, every time.

And their talk was as simple, as eager, as unaffected, as hers had been as she talked with Godmother about her blue silk dress. All those things were a part of their world, as the blue dress was a part of hers.

She was so interested that she forgot to be afraid. And by and by when God-mother had drifted off with some one and Mary Alice found herself alone with one man, she was feeling so "folksy" that she looked up at him and laughed.

"Seems as if every one had found a 'burning theme'—all but us!" she said.

The young man—he *was* young, and very good-looking, in an unusual sort of way—flushed. "I don't know any of them," he said; "I'm a stranger."

"So am I," said Mary Alice, "and I don't know any one either. But I'd like to know some of these people better; wouldn't you?"

"I don't know," returned the young man. "I haven't seen much of people, and I don't feel at home with them."

"Oh!" cried Mary Alice, quite excitedly, "you need a fairy godmother to tell you a Secret."

The young man looked unpleasantly mystified. "What secret?" he asked.

She started to explain. He seemed amused, at first, in a supercilious kind of way. But Mary Alice was so interested in her "burning theme" that she did not notice how he looked. Gradually his superciliousness faded.

"Let us find a place where you can tell me the Secret," he said, looking about the drawing-room. Every place seemed taken.

"There's a settle in the hall," suggested

Mary Alice. And they went out and sat on that. "But I can't tell you the Secret," she said. "Not yet, anyway."

"Please!" he begged. "I may never see you again."

She looked distressed. "Oh, do you think so?" she said. "But anyhow I can't tell you. I can only tell you up to where the Secret comes in, and then—if I never see you again, you can think about it; and any time you write to me for the Secret, I'll send it to you to help you when you need it most."

"I need it now," he urged.

"No, you don't," she answered. "I thought I needed it right away, but I wouldn't have understood it or believed it if I'd heard it then." And she told him how it was whispered to her, after she had been kind to the man of many millions.

"And does it work?" he asked, laughing at her story of the toast and tea.

"I don't know, yet," she admitted, "I'm just trying it. That's another reason I can't tell you now. I have to wait until I've tried it thoroughly."

"You're a nice, modest young person from the backwoods," laughed Godmother when they were going home, "selecting the largest, livest lion of the evening and running off with him to the safe shelter of the hall."

"Lion?" said Mary Alice, wonderingly. "What lion?"

"The young man you kept so shamelessly to yourself nearly all evening."

"I didn't know he was any kind of a lion," apologized Mary Alice, humbly. "He just seemed to be ——" She stopped, and her eyes danced delightedly. "I was

[64]

trying the Secret on him," she went on, "and I believe it worked."

"I think it must have," said Godmother, "for he came up to me, before I left, and exhibited all the signs of a gentleman who wants to be asked to call. So I invited him to come in to-morrow for a cup of tea."

"Is he—is he coming?" asked Mary Alice, "and won't you please tell me what kind of a lion he is, and what's his name?"

"He is coming," said Godmother, smiling mischievously, "and I don't know whether to tell you his name or not. Maybe he'd rather do that himself."

"I don't care if he doesn't," laughed Mary Alice; "he's a nice man, and he seemed to be real——" And then she stopped again and looked mysteriously knowing. And Godmother nodded approvingly.

[65]

"I loved the party," murmured Mary Alice, happily, as Godmother bent over to give her her last good-night kiss. "I never supposed a party where one didn't know a soul could be so nice."

"Knowing or not knowing people makes much less difference—when you remember the Secret. Don't you find it so?" said Godmother.

And Mary Alice assented. "Yes, oh, yes! It's a wonderful magic—the dear Secret is," she said.

VII

AT CANDLE-LIGHTIN' TIME

THE next morning, Mary Alice wanted to know who everybody was; and Godmother told her—every one but "the young man lion" as she called him. The home they had been to was that of a celebrated editor and man of letters who numbered among his friends the most delightful people of many nations. The guests represented a variety of talents. The large, dark, distinctly-foreign looking man was the great baritone of one of the opera houses. The younger man, with the long, dark hair, was a violinist about whom all New York was talking. The gray-haired man with the goatee was an admiral. The gentle-spoken, shy man with the silver hair was a famous Indian fighter

of the old frontier days. The man who
spoke informedly of the Children's Theatre was one of the best-known of Ameri-
can men of letters. The lady who was
anxious to interrogate him about it was
one whose fame as an uplifter of humanity has travelled 'round the globe.
This one was a painter, and that one a
sculptor, and another was a poetic dram-
atist.

"My!" sighed Mary Alice, "I'm glad
you *didn't* tell me before we went. As
nearly as I can remember, I talked to the
Admiral about the Fifth Avenue shop-
windows, and to the General about the
Jumel Mansion—which he said he had
never seen but had always meant to see
—and to the painter—what *did* I talk to
the painter about? Oh! my pink beads.
He admired the colour."

"Yes," said Godmother, "and if you

had known who they were you would probably have tried to talk to the Admiral about ships and sea-fights, and to the painter about the Metropolitan Museum, and would have bored them terribly. Most real people, I think, like to be taken for what they are rather than for what they may have done. That is one of the things I learned in my long years in Europe where I was constantly finding myself in conversation with some one I did not know. We always began on a basis of common humanity, and we soon found our mutual interests, and enjoyed talking about them. It taught me a great deal about people and the folly of taking any of them on other people's estimates."

But all this was only mildly interesting, now, compared with "the young man lion."

[69]

Of course they had to tell him, first thing when he came, that Mary Alice did not know who he was. He looked a little surprised at first; then he seemed to relish the joke hugely. When God-mother added certain explanations, he grew grave again.

"I like that," he said. "I think it's a fine game, and I wish I might play it. I can't, most of the time. But I can play it with you, if you'll let me," he went on, turning to Mary Alice. She nodded assent. "That's splendid!" he cried. "I haven't played a jolly game like this since I was a boy. Now, you're not to think I'm a king in disguise or anything like that. There's really nothing about me that's at all interesting; only, on account of something that has happened to me, people are talking about me—for nine days or so. I'll be going on, in a day or two, and every one will forget. Now let's play the game. May I make toast?"

"You may," she said.

In a little while, some one came to call on Godmother who took the caller into the library; and the toast-making went on undisturbed.

Whoever he was, he seemed to know something about camp-fires; and squatting on the rug before the glowing grate, toasting bread, reminded him of things he had heard strange men tell, as the intimacy of the night fire in the wilderness brought their stories out. It was fascinating talk, and Mary Alice listened enthralled.

"I didn't know I had that much talk in me," he laughed, a little confusedly, as he rose to go. "It must be the surroundings that are responsible—and the game."

[71]

Godmother, whose caller was gone, asked him to stay to dinner.

"I wish I could!" he said wistfully, noting in the distance the cozy dinner table set for two. "If you could only know where I must dine instead!"

"You seem to dread it," said Mary Alice.

"I do," he answered.

She looked at Godmother. "I wish we could tell him the Secret," she suggested shyly, "it might help."

Godmother looked very thoughtful, as if gravely considering. "Not yet," she decided, shaking her head; "it's too soon."

"I think so too," he said. "I'm afraid you might lose interest in me after you had told me. I'd rather wait."

The next day was Sunday. He had

engagements for lunch and dinner, but he asked if he might slip in again for tea; he was leaving town Monday.

So they had another beautiful hour, at what Godmother loved to speak of as "candle-lightin' time," and while Mary Alice was in the kitchen cutting bread to toast, Godmother and her guest made notes in tiny note-books.

"There!" she said, when she had written the Gramercy Park address in his book. "Anything you send here will always reach her, wherever she is."

"And any answer she may care to make to me, if you'll address it to me there," handing back her book to her, "will always reach me, wherever I may be."

"It is a splendid game," he said when he was going, "and I'm glad you let me

[73]

play. If more people played this game,
I'd find the world a lot pleasanter place
to live in."

"When you know the Secret you can
show other people how to play," Mary
Alice suggested.

"That's so," he said. "Well, I shan't
let you forget you are to tell it to me."

VIII

LEARNING TO BE BRAVE AND SWEET

GODMOTHER'S charming drawing-room seemed intolerably empty when he had gone and they two stood by the fire and looked into it trying to see again the jungle scene he had pointed out to them in the bed of coals. But the jungle was gone; the vision had faded with the seer. And Godmother and Mary Alice began picking up the teacups and the toast plate, almost as if there had been a funeral.

Then Godmother laughed. "How solemn we are!" she said, pretending to think it all very funny.

But Mary Alice couldn't pretend. She set down his teacup which she had just lifted with gentle reverence off the mantel,

where he left it, and went closer to Godmother. Her lips were trembling, but
she did not have to speak.

"I know, Precious—I know," whispered Godmother. She sat down in a
big chair close to the fire—the chair he
had just left—and Mary Alice sat on the
hearth-rug and nestled her head against
Godmother's knees. Neither of them
said anything for what seemed a long
time. They just looked into the glowing
bed of coals and saw—different things!

Then, "I think," Mary Alice began, in
a voice that was full of tears, "I think I
wish we hadn't played any game. I
think I wish I hadn't seen him at all."

"Lovey *dear!*"

"Yes, I do!" wept Mary Alice, refus-
ing to be comforted. "Everything was
beautiful, before he came. And now he's
gone, and I'm so—lonesome!"

[76]

Godmother was silent for a moment. "There's the Secret," she suggested, at last. "It was—it was when I felt just as you do now, that I began to learn the Secret."

Mary Alice made no reply; there seemed to be nothing that she could say But after they had sat silent for a long while, she got up and kissed her godmother with a new passion which had in it tenderness as well as adoration.

"I don't believe I can be brave and lovely about it, as you must have been to make people love you so. But I'm going to *try*," she said.

The success with which Mary Alice's trying met was really beautiful to see. At first, it was pretty hard for her to care much about the Secret, or about people. Every assemblage just seemed to her an empty crowd where he was not. But

when she began to wonder to how many
of those selfsame people the others
seemed the same as to her, she was interested once more ; the Secret began to
work.

It worked so well, in fact, that Mary
Alice came to be quite famous in a small
way. People in Godmother's distin-
guished and delightful " set " talked en-
thusiastically of Mary Alice's quiet
charm, and she was asked here and
asked there, and had a quite wonderful
time.

Her " poor " friend came in, whenever
he could, for tea and toast ; and sometimes he made what he called " a miser-
able return " for this hospitality, by ask-
ing Godmother and Mary Alice to dine
with him at his palace on upper Fifth
Avenue and afterwards to sit in his box
at the opera. He was a widower, and

his two sons were married and lived in palaces of their own. His only daughter was abroad finishing her education; and his great, lonely house was to serve a brief purpose for her when she "came out" and until she married. Then, he thought, he would either give it up or turn it over to her; certainly he would not keep it for himself.

At first, Mary Alice found it hard to remember the Secret "with so many foot-men around." But by and by she got used to them and, other things being equal, could have nearly as good a time in a palace as in a flat. For this, she had a wonderful example in Godmother of whom some one had once said, admir-ingly, that she was "never mean to any-body just because he's rich." It was true. Godmother was just as "nice" to the rich as to the poor, to the "cowering celebrity " (as she was wont to say) as to the most important nobody. It was the Secret that helped her to do it. It was the Secret that helped Mary Alice.

And so the winter went flying by. Twice, letters came—from him ; and Mary Alice answered them, giving the answers to Godmother to send. Once he wrote from London, and once from somewhere on the Bosphorus. They were lonesome letters, both ; but he didn't ask for the Secret, though he mentioned it each time.

IX

TELLING THE SECRET TO MOTHER

In March, Godmother said: "I am going abroad for the summer, dear, and I've just had a conference with my man of affairs. He reports some unexpectedly good dividends from my small handful of stock in a company that is enjoying a boom, and so if we're careful—you and I —there will be enough so I can take you with me." Mary Alice was too surprised, too happy to speak. "Now, you'll want to go home, of course," Godmother went on, "and so we'll agree on a sailing date and then you may fly back to mother as soon as you wish, and stay till it's time to go abroad."

They decided to sail the first of May; so Mary Alice went home almost immediately, and on an evening late in March got off the train on to that familiar plat-form whence she had so fearfully set forth only four short months ago.

Father was at the station to meet her; and at home, by the soft-coal fire burning beneath the white marble mantel in the sitting-room, Mother was sewing and waiting for her.

Mary Alice was thinking, as she and Father neared the house, of that miser-able evening in the fall when she had stolen past her mother and gone up to her room and wept passionately, in the dark, because life had no enchantment for her. There would be no stealing past dear Mother now! For the Secret was for Mother, too—yes, very much in-deed for Mother, as Mary Alice and God-mother had agreed in their wonderful "tucking in" talk the night before Mary

Telling the Secret to Mother

Alice came away. All the way home, on the train, she had hardly been able to wait till she got to Mother with this beautiful new thing in her heart.

Perhaps Mother had dreaded her girl's home-coming, in a way, almost as much as she yearned for it. But if she had, Mary Alice never knew it; and if she had, Mother herself soon forgot it. For in all the twenty years of Mary Alice's life, her mother had never, it seemed, had so much of her girl as in the month that followed her home-coming. Hour after hour they worked about the house or sat before that grate fire in the unchanged sitting-room, and talked and talked and talked. Mary Alice told every little detail of those four months until her mother lived them over with her and the light and life of them animated her as they had animated Mary Alice.

Little by little, in that month, Mary Alice came at least to the beginning of a wonderful new understanding : came to see how parents—and *god*parents !— cease to have any particular future of their own and live in the futures of the young things they love. Mary Alice's bleak years had been bitter for her mother, too; perhaps bitterer than for her. And her new enchantment with life was like new blood in her mother's veins.

Mother cried when Mary Alice told her the Secret. "Oh, it's true! it's true!" she said. "If only everybody could know it, what a different world this would be!"

And as for the—Other! When Mary Alice told her mother about him and what his coming into her life and his going out of it had meant, Mother just held her girl close and could not speak.

The precious month flew by on wings as of the wind. Mary Alice was "the town wonder," as her brother Johnny said, and she enjoyed that as only a girl who has been the town wall-flower can; but after all, everything was as nothing compared with Mother and the exultation that had so evidently come into her life because out of her love and pain and sacrifice a soul had come into the world to draw so richly from the treasures of other hearts and to give so richly back again. There is no triumph like it, as Mary Alice would perhaps know, some day. A mother's purest happiness is very like God's own.

But at last the sailing date was close at hand. Mary Alice's heart was heavy and glad together. "If I could only take you!" she whispered to her mother.

Mother shook her head. "I wouldn't go and leave your father and the children," she said. "You go and enjoy it all for me. I like it better that way."

And so, once more Mary Alice smiled through tear-filled eyes at the dear faces on the station platform, and was gone again into the big world beyond her home. But this time what a different girl it was who went!

X

THE OLD WORLD AND THE KING

THEY had an unusually delightful voyage. The weather was perfection and their fellow-voyagers included many persons interesting to talk with and many others interesting to observe and speculate about.

One particularly charming experience came to Mary Alice through the Captain's appreciation of her eagerness. Godmother had taught her to love the stars. As well as they could, in New York where, to most people, only scraps of sky are visible at a time, they had been wont to watch with keen interest for the nightly appearance of stars they could see from their windows or from the streets as they went to and fro. And

when they got aboard ship and had the
whole sky to look at, they revelled in
their night hours on the deck, and in
picking out the constellations and their
" bright, particular stars." This led the
Captain to tell Mary Alice something of
the stars as the sailors' friends ; and she
had one of the most memorable evenings
of her life when he explained to her something of the science of navigation and
made her see how their great greyhound
of the ocean, just like the first frail barks
of the Tyrians, picked its way across
trackless wastes of sea by the infallible
guidance of " the friendly stars." All
this particularly interested Mary Alice
because of Some One who lived much in
the open and spent many and many a
night on the broad deserts, looking up at
the stars.

They landed at Naples, and lingered a

fortnight in that lovely vicinity ; then, up to Rome, to Florence and Venice, to Milan and the Italian Lakes, through Switzerland into France, and so to Paris. Godmother had once spent a winter at Capri ; she had spent several winters in Florence. She knew Venice well. She had hosts of dear, familiar things to show Mary Alice in each place.

At last they came to Paris. Godmother lamented that it was in July they came ; but Mary Alice, who had no recollections of Paris in April and May, found nothing to lament. They stayed more than a month—and made a number of the enchanting little journeys which can be made out of Paris forever and ever without repeating, it seems.

Then, with a trunk in which were two " really, truly " Paris dresses—very, very modest ones, to be sure, but unmis-

takably touched with Parisian *chic*—and a
mind in which were hundreds of wonderful Paris memories, Mary Alice crossed
to England. They went at once to London where, it seemed to Mary Alice, she
must stay forever, to be satisfied. Godmother had hosts of charming friends in
London, even beyond what she had in
Italy and France; but for the first fortnight she gave up her time entirely to
Mary Alice's sightseeing. By and by
her friends began to find out she was
there and to clamour insistently for her.
And as the exodus from town was as
complete as it ever gets, most of the invitations were from the country. So that
Mary Alice began to see something of
that English country-house life she had
read so much about, and to meet personages whose names filled her with awe
—until she remembered the Secret. And

thus she came to the Great Event of her
life.

Godmother had what Mary Alice called
"a duchess friend" of whom she was
very, very fond. The Duchess was a
woman about Godmother's age, and quite
as lovely to look at as a duchess should
be. She was mistress of many and vast
estates, and wore—on occasions—a coro-
net of diamonds and strings of pearls
"worth a king's ransom," just like a
duchess in a story. But she seemed to
Mary Alice to have hardly the mildest
interest in the jewels she wore and the
palaces she lived in ; Mary Alice found it
hard to bear in mind that to the Duchess
these were just as matter-of-fact, as usual,
as unvariable, as the home sitting-room
and the "good" hat had once been to
Mary Alice. And like Mary Alice, the
Duchess found her happiness in reaching

out for something new and different. The
Duchess liked the world that Godmother
lived in—the world of Godmother's lovely
mind; and she loved Godmother's companionship.

That was how it came about that Mary
Alice found herself very often in exalted
society. The exalted personages did not
notice her much; but every once in a
while, by remembering the Secret, she
got on happy terms with some of them.

And at last a very unusual thing happened. The King was coming to honour
the Duke and Duchess with a visit;
coming to see one of those ancient and
glorious estates the like of which no king
owns, and which are the pride of all the
kingdom. Many sovereigns had stayed
at this splendid old place on England's
south coast—a place as famous for its
beauty as for its six hundred years of

history ; so it was no unusual thing for it to house a king The unusual part of it all was Mary Alice being there. By the King's permission a wonderful house party was asked to meet him. Godmother couldn't be asked ; she had never been presented, and the King was unaware of her existence. The Duchess would not have dared to present Godmother's name on the list submitted to the King. Much less, therefore, would she have dared to present Mary Alice's. " But —— ! " said the Duchess, and went on to unfold a plan.

If Mary Alice would not mind staying on with the Duchess while Godmother paid another visit ; and if she would not mind having a room somewhere in a remote wing ; and would not mind not being asked to mingle with the party in any way, she might see something of such sights as perhaps she would never be able to see otherwise. Mary Alice was delighted partly because she wanted to see the sights and partly because the thought of going away from this wonderful place made her heart ache. So she was moved out of the fine guest suite she and Godmother had been lodged in, and over to a room in a far wing of the vast house. From this wing one could look down on to the terraces for which the love and genius of none other than quaint John Evelyn—greatest of England's Garden Philosophers—were responsible. To these terraces the guests would certainly come, and to the world-famous rose garden into which also Mary Alice could look from her window in the far wing. But even if she were to see no royalty, she was grateful for the privilege of staying on a few days longer in this

The Old World and the King

Paradise by the sea. And not the least
delight of her new quarters was that they
were high enough up so that from them
she could overlook the sheltering Ilex-
trees which made these marvellous gardens possible so close to the shore, and see
the Channel ships a-sailing—three-masted
schooners laden with wood; fishing-
smacks; London barges with their pic-
turesque red sails bellying in the wind;
and an occasional ocean liner trailing its
black smoke across the horizon. What
with the sea and the gardens and the
rich history of the place, Mary Alice felt
that she could never tire of it, even if she
did not see the King. But it would be
delightful to see him, too. Some day
the history of this splendid old place
would include this royal visit; and Mary
Alice, who had read of other such occasions and wished she might have been

a mouse in a corner to witness them—
as, for instance, when Queen Elizabeth
was here—now felt the thrill of having
that wish come true, in a way ; and so
far from feeling "set aside" or slighted,
liked her window in the wing and her
participation in the party above any other
she might have had.

Mary Alice dined, the first night of the
house party, with the Duchess's older
children, and then went back to her room
to sit at the window and look down on the
terraces where, after a while, some of the
men guests came to smoke.

It was late, but the twilight still lingered. Mary Alice could not tell who
many of the men were, but she could see
the King and she watched him interestedly
as he paced up and down. She had been
told how no one must speak to a king
until the king has first spoken to him ;

and she felt that at best it must be a dreary business—being a king.

Presently, though, in the thickening shadows she saw a form that made her heart stand still. *Could it be?* She was probably mistaken—madly mistaken— but something in the way a man down there carried himself made her think of Godmother's little drawing-room in far-off New York and a man who was " playing the game." But the King was talking to this man—talking most interestedly, it seemed. She *must* be mistaken !

Nevertheless, when the men had all gone in, she put on a white shawl and slipped down on to the terrace. She felt as if she must know ; and of course she couldn't ask, for she did not know his name.

The terraces were deserted, and she paced up and down undisturbed, trying to assure herself that Godmother would probably have known if he were in England—his last letter had been from the Far East—and especially if he were coming here. There were times, as she reminded herself, when she was continually seeing him ; out of every crowd, suddenly his tall form would seem to emerge; in the loneliness of quiet places, as by miracle he would seem to be where a moment ago she knew there was no one. Then a sense of separation would intervene, and for days she would be given over to the belief that she was never to see him again. To-night was doubtless just one of the times when, for no reason that she could understand, he seemed physically near to her.

She was standing very still in the shadow of an ivy-grown pillar, looking up at the Pole star and wondering if he in his wanderings might not be looking at it too, when a man's voice close beside her made her jump. It was an unfamiliar voice. "Star-gazing?" it said, pleasantly. She turned, and recognized the King.

"Yes, Your Majesty," she answered. At first she thought she was going to be frightened. Then she remembered the Secret, and before she knew it she was deep in conversation with the King.

As she talked, a puzzled expression she could not see came into the King's face. He had a wonderful memory for names, a memory which seldom failed him; but he couldn't place this girl. And it was dark, too, so he couldn't see her. But he liked to hear her talk. She had that rare thing, in his experience, a fresh, sweet view-point. The bloom of enchantment was still on life for her, and as he drew

[99]

her out, he found that she was refreshing him as nothing had done for a weary while.

Then, kingly obligation called him indoors to join the throng whose everlasting sameness palled on him almost unendurably. Something he said made Mary Alice feel this—made her see, as in a flash, a girl who had gone home, once, from a party and wept because life was so dull. She was sorry for the King!

"I seldom forget a name," he said, "but I—before we go in, won't you please remind me of yours?"

Mary Alice laughed. "Your Majesty has never heard my name," she said, "and I can't go in; I'm not of the party." And she explained.

"I see," he said. "I shall have to thank the Duchess. I have had a most refreshing quarter of an hour."

"I'm glad," said Mary Alice, simply.
"I felt afraid, at first—as nearly everybody does, I suppose. And then I
thought how dreadful that must be—to
have every one afraid of you, when
you're really a very nice, gentle person
—I mean ——! Well, I guess Your Majesty knows what I mean. And then I
remembered my Secret ——"

"Secret?"

And so, of course, she had to tell. It
was rather a long story, hurry as she
would, because the King interrupted
with so many questions. But she
wouldn't tell what the Secret was until
"the very last thing."

"Um," said the King, when she had
finally divulged it. That was all he said;
but the way he said it made Mary Alice
know that the Secret was right.

XI

A MEETING AND A PARTING

THE next day was full of activities which kept the house guests far afield. But Mary Alice had an exciting day at home; for the King had spoken to the Duchess about her and asked to have her presented to him that evening.

The Duke and Duchess had spent a fortune on the entertainment of their King; had provided for his beguiling every costly diversion that could be thought of. But they had not been able to give him anything new, and they felt that he was enduring the visit amiably rather than actually enjoying it. It remained, apparently, for the Girl from Nowhere to give him real pleasure.

" . . . found herself looking into eyes that smiled as with
an old friendliness."

(*Page 103*)

A Meeting and a Parting

So the Duchess—secretly sympathetic
—left orders with her French maid that
Mary Alice was to be made ready to
see the King.

Mary Alice chose the simplest thing
that rigorous French maid would allow
and kept as close as possible to her own
individual and unpretending style. But
even then, she was a pretty resplendent
young person as she stole timidly down
to find the Duchess and be presented to
the King.

The guests were assembled in the
great drawing-room, and Mary Alice
was frightened almost to death when
she saw the splendour of the scene and
realized what part she had to play in it.

Then, in a daze, she was swept forward
and presented, and found herself looking into eyes that smiled as with an old
friendliness. So she smiled back again,

and soon forgot the onlookers, answering
His Majesty's kindly questions.

He turned from her, presently, to speak
to some one else, and Mary Alice caught
sight then of a face she knew. For an
instant, she stood staring. For an instant, he stood staring back, as unbeliev-
ing as she.

Then, "You seem to be on friendly
terms with His Majesty," he said. "Have
you showed him how to play the game,
too?"

"No," Mary Alice answered, "but
I've told him the Secret."

As soon as they could, they escaped—
those two—out on to the terrace where
the stars were shining thickly overhead.

"On one of those—those times in New
York when we talked together," he said,
"you told me that when something very

marvellous had happened to you and you couldn't believe you were awake, that it was really true, you asked your Godmother to pinch you. It—er, wouldn't be at all proper for me to ask you to please pinch me. But if you know any perfectly proper equivalent, I wish you'd do it."

"I've pinched myself," she returned, "and it seems I am awake. So I judge you must be, too."

"Then how, please——?"

And she told him.

"And you don't know yet who I am?"

"No."

So he told her. "I warned you it was nothing interesting," he said; "it is just my work that people are interested in. I don't belong in there," indicating the great house, "any more than you do. They like me for a novelty, because I've dared and suffered; and because, as things turned out, I was in a position to do what they are pleased to call a great service to the Empire. I wish I liked them better—they want to be very kind to me, and I was born of them, so they like me the better for that. But I've been in the wilderness too much—I can't get used to these strange folk at home."

"I used to think I couldn't get used to strange folk," Mary Alice murmured, "but I seem to have got on fairly well for a girl from Nowhere."

"Was it the Secret?"

She nodded.

"When may I know?"

"I—I can't tell."

"You told the King."

"He seemed to need it so."

"Don't I need it?"

"I—I can't tell."

A Meeting and a Parting

He seemed discouraged, and as if he did not know what next to say. They strolled in silence over to where she had been standing the night before when the King spoke to her. From within the great house came the entrancingly sweet song of a world-famous soprano engaged to pour her liquid notes before the King.

Mary Alice stood very still, drinking it in. When it ceased, she stole a look up at the bronzed face beside her; the light from a window in her far wing of the house fell full on that rugged face, and it looked very stern but also very sad. Mary Alice's heart, which had been exultant only a short while ago, began suddenly—in one of those strange revulsions which all hearts know—to ache indefinably. This hour would probably be like those other brief hours in which he had shared her life. To-morrow, or next day, he would be gone; and forever and forever the memory of these moments on the terrace, with the stars overhead and that exquisite song in their ears, would be coming back to taunt her unbearably.

She made up her mind that before he went out of her life again, she would tell him the Secret; so that at least, wherever he went, however far from him the rest of her way through life might lie, they would always have that thought in common; and whenever it came to help him, as it must, he would think of her.

Timidly she laid a hand upon his arm. He had been far away, following the trail of long, long thoughts, and her touch recalled him sharply.

"What is it?" he asked.

"I—I want to tell you the Secret."

"I don't think I want to know," he answered, rather shortly.

A Meeting and a Parting

"Why—why ——" Mary Alice faltered. Her lips quivered and her eyes began to fill. "I—I must go in," she said.

He put out a hand to detain her, but either she did not see it in the dark, or else she eluded it; for in a moment she was gone, across the terrace towards the lighted French windows of the rooms of state.

How she managed to get through those next few minutes until she could find the Duchess and ask to be excused, Mary Alice never knew. All of her that was capable of feeling or caring about anything seemed to have left this part of her that wore the Duchess's lovely white gown and scarf of silver tissue, and to be out on the dark terrace under the pale star beams, with a tall young man who spoke bitterly. This girl in the sheen of white and silver to whom the King was speaking kindly, was some one unreal and ghostly who acted like a real live girl, but was not.

As she hurried along the great corridors towards her room in the far wing, Mary Alice felt that she could hardly wait to get off these trappings of state; to get back to her old simple self again and bury her head in her pillow and cry and cry. She wished with all her heart for God-mother. But most of all she was sick for home, for Mother, and the unchanging sitting-room.

"He" had seemed disappointed to find her here. And she——? Well! she was sorry she had seen him. In New York, where she had not even known his name, he had seemed to belong to her, in a way, by right of their common sympathy and understanding. Here, among all these people who were his people, who delighted to honour him, he seemed completely lost to her. . . .

After a weary while, Mary Alice got up and sat by the window, looking across to the main part of the great house and wondering which of the darkened windows was his and if he had dismissed her easily from his mind and gone comfortably to sleep. The early dawn breeze was blowing from the sea when she dozed into a brief, dream-troubled sleep.

XII

AT OCEAN'S EDGE

ONLY the gardeners and a few of the house servants were about when she went down-stairs, through the still house and out on to the terraces, towards the sea. She had hung the white and silver finery carefully away, glad to feel so far divorced from it and all it represented as she did in her gown of unbleached linen crash which she and Godmother had made.

" I'm like Cinderella," she reminded herself as she buttoned the crash gown, " Godmother and all. Only, her prince loved her when he saw her in her finery, and mine despised me. I suppose he thought I was a silly little ' climber ' trying to get out of the chimney-corner where I belong. But I think he owed it to me to let me explain."

There was a cove on the shore whose shelter she particularly loved; and she was going thither now, as these bitter reflections filled her mind. The tide was ebbing, but the thin, slowly-widening line of beach was wet and she had to pick her way carefully. She was so mindful of her steps and, under all her mindfulness, so conscious of the ache in her heart, that she was not noticing much else than the way to pick her steps; and she had rounded the rocky corner of the cove and was far into her favoured little nook, when she saw that it was occupied. A man sat back in its deepest shelter, looking out to sea. He started when he saw her, and she looked back as if calculating a flight.

"Please don't go," he begged, rising

to greet her. " I was unpardonably rude to you last night and it has made me very wretched. You have no right to pardon me, but I hope you won't go away without letting me tell you how sorry I am."

" I—it was nothing—I pardon you—I think I understand," said Mary Alice, weakly.

He shook his head. " How could you —who are so gentle—understand?" Mary Alice looked about to protest, but he silenced her with a commanding gesture. " I've been so much with savages that I've grown savage in my own ways, it seems. But—it was like this: You taught me a game, once. It was a charming game and I was glad to learn. But we could play it only twice, and then I had to go away. And after I went I—I was always missing the game, always wanting to play again. At what you called 'candle-lightin' time,' wherever I was—in strange drawing-rooms, on rushing express trains, on ships plowing the seas, sitting about camp-fires in the wilderness—I'd always seem to see that little, dim-lit room in your New York, and you kneeling beside me on the hearth-rug, with the firelight on your face and hair. I've always been a lonely chap; but after that I was lonelier than ever; I used to think I couldn't bear it. Then last night—how shall I tell you how I felt? I've comforted myself, before, with the dream that some day I might get back to New York, to that little room at candle-lightin' time, and find you again, and forget everything in all the world but that you were there and I was with you, kneeling on the hearth-rug and making toast for tea. And when I saw you, all white and silver glitter, talking to the King—the dream was gone. There wasn't any girl on the hearth-rug in New York ; there was only another girl of the kind that always makes me feel so strange, so ill at ease. It was only night before last that I learned I am to go away again directly, to the Far East, for the Government; and I was so happy, for I thought I'd go the westward way and see you again in New York. Then, suddenly, I realized that you were gone— not merely from New York, but from the dream. And I was surprised into rudeness. That's all. But *please* forgive me ! "

"I told you I understood," said Mary Alice, "and in a way I did—not that the —the dream as you call it meant so much to you, but that you were disappointed to find Cinderella come out of her chimney corner and talking to the King. I know that when we have a person definitely placed in our minds, we don't like to have him bob up suddenly in quite another quarter and in what seems like quite another character."

"Not if that person has been a kind of —of lode-star to you, and you have been steering your course by—by her," he said.

Mary Alice flushed. "Now I think you ought to let *me* tell," she began, with downcast eyes. And so she told: how she had come there, and how she had stayed, like the little mouse under the Queen's chair, and how glad she was to have seen from a distance a little of this splendour and great society, and how gladder still to hang her borrowed white and silver away and be done with it and all it stood for and go back to her gown of crash and her chimney-corner place in life, "which I can now see," she added, "is the place for dreams and sweet companionship."

"And when I get back, will you be there?" he cried, eagerly.

"When you get back I will be there," she promised.

After that they sat and talked for long and long, while the blue sea sparkled in the summer morning sun. When, at length, they rose to go, there was a light that never shone on land or sea in his face and in hers. There had been no further promises; only that one: "When you get back I will be there." But each heart understood the other, and she re joiced to wait further declaration of his love until he could, according to his tender fancy, make it to her as in his "dream come true."

On the beach as they strolled back, it was her eyes—shining with a soft, new radiance—that first caught sight of something; her fancy that first grasped its significance. "Look!" she cried. In a bowl-like hollow of a big brown rock, the receding tide had left a little pool of sea-water. "It's left behind—this bit of the infinite, unresting sea!" she said. "Who knows what far, far shores it's come from? And now, here it is, and the great mother-sea's gone off and left it."

He smiled tenderly at her sweet whimsy. "The great mother-sea will come back for it at sundown," he reminded her.

"Yes—yes"—perhaps it was the coming separation between the two that made her voice quaver so sympathetically—"the Infinite always comes back for us. But we don't always remember that it will! This is such a little bit of

the great sea. Maybe it never was left
alone before ; maybe it doesn't know how
surely the waters that left it behind will
come back for it this evening. Maybe
it's—it's lonesome. I—I think I know
how it feels."

" And I," he said.

" Next time you feel that way will you
remember this brown rock and the tide
that is so surely coming back to-
night ?" she asked.

" Indeed I will," he told her.

" And so will I," she went on. " And
I'll try to remember, too, that perhaps it
was put here for us to see and think
of when we need encouragement—just
as, I dare say, we are left behind, sometimes, so that other lonely folk may see
us and be reminded that ——" She
stopped.

" That what ?" he asked.

"Why!" she cried, "it's the Secret! The more you live, the more everything helps you to believe the Secret and to feel the brotherhood it brings."

He looked guilty. "I don't deserve to know the Secret," he said, "after last night. But——"

"But I am going to tell you," she declared, "so when you're far away from what you love most, or when you're with people you think are different from you and do not understand, you can remember——"

"Yes?" eagerly.

"Just remember—and you've no idea how it helps until you've tried—that *everybody 's lonesome.* That's the Secret."

10   PRINTED IN THE UNITED STATES OF AMERICA